New School For Mouse

WRITTEN BY

Fynisa Engler

ILLUSTRATED BY

Ryan Law

This edition first published in 2023
by Lawley Publishing,
a division of Lawley Enterprises LLC

Text Copyright © 2023 by Fynisa Engler
Illustration Copyright © 2023 by Ryan Law
All Rights Reserved

Hardcover ISBN 978-1-958302-39-2
Paperback ISBN 978-1-958302-41-5
Library of Congress Control Number: 2022948370

Lawley Publishing
70 S. Val Vista Dr. #A3 #188
Gilbert, AZ 85296
LawleyPublishing.com

LAWLEY
PUBLISHING

Mouse stared out the school bus window. It felt like butterflies were fluttering in his stomach. "I want to go to my old school," he said. But it was too far away.

"I was really nervous on my first day too," said Hedgehog. "But I made new friends."

Today was Mouse's first day at his new school since moving in with Mama Bunny, Hedgehog, and the other foster children. Mouse's mom wasn't able to take care of him, so he had come to live at Mama Bunny's foster home.

He thought about his mom and his best friend, Otter. He missed them both so much. *What if no one at the new school wants to be my friend?* Mouse worried.

When they arrived at school, Hedgehog helped Mouse find his class. "Don't forget, we ride bus 24. I'll see you after school," Hedgehog said.

"Wait, what about lunch?" Mouse asked nervously. "I'll see you at lunch, right?"

"No, we're in different grade so we eat at different times.'

The butterflies started fluttering in Mouse's stomach again, and he began to panic. "Who will I sit with?" he asked. "You'll be okay," Hedgehog said, turning to go to class.

Mouse's new teacher, Ms. Peacock, introduced him to the class. Mouse looked around, hoping to make a new friend.

During reading time when they needed partners, everyone already had a friend, so Mouse had to work with Ms. Peacock.

At recess, there were kids playing on the monkey bars. When Mouse asked if he could play with them, they ran away. *I'm never going to make a new friend,* Mouse thought as a tear slid down his face.

During math, Mouse thought about his old school and his friend, Otter. Otter would trade Mouse his granola bar for Mouse's pudding. He wondered if Otter had made a new friend.

$2+1=3$
$2+2=4$
$2+3=5$
$2+4=6$
$2+5=7$
$2+6=8$
$2+7=9$
$2+8=10$
$2+9=11$
$2+10=12$

A loud buzz startled Mouse.
The other kids cheered and stood up.

"Mouse, that's the lunch bell. Line up at the door and we'll walk to the cafeteria," Ms. Peacock said. The butterflies fluttered worse than ever.

At the cafeteria, Mouse got his tray of food and slowly walked past each table. No one smiled at him. No one waved him over.

In the corner, someone was sitting alone. Mouse saw the name Rabbit written on his lunch bag. *Here's my chance,* Mouse thought.

As Mouse sat at the lunch table,
Rabbit looked up, startled.
"Hi, I'm Mouse."

Rabbit smiled and waved.
He pointed to his name
on his bag.

"Want my applesauce?" Mouse asked.

Rabbit stared at him and seemed confused.

Mouse asked again, pointing to his applesauce.
Rabbit nodded, then reached into his lunch bag and
pulled out two cookies. He gave one cookie to Mouse.
"Hey, thanks," Mouse said.

Rabbit took out a note
and showed it to Mouse:

After lunch, Mouse followed Rabbit out to the playground.
"Do you want to be my friend?" Mouse asked.
Rabbit smiled and nodded.

Rabbit taught Mouse
the sign for 'friends.'

Every day, Mouse was excited to see Rabbit at lunch.

One day, Rabbit was teaching Mouse new signs when someone walked by with a lunch tray, looking as nervous as Mouse was on his first day.

Remembering how alone he'd felt, Mouse smiled.
"You can sit with us," he called, waving him over.

It felt good to help someone else. And quickly, the three became best friends.

CPSIA information can be obtained
at www.ICGtesting.com
Printed in the USA
LVHW072015200723
752770LV00004B/148